NINE LIVES

THE RETURN OF

DAISY, BUTTERCUP AND WEED

LUCY DANIELS

Nine Lives

The Return of Daisy, Buttercup and Weed

Illustrated by Bill Geldart

Hodder Children's Books

a division of Hodder Headline Limited

Special thanks to Andrea Abbott

First published in Great Britain in 2001
by Hodder Children's Books

10 9 8 7 6 5 4 3 2 1

A Catalogue record for this book is available from the British Library

ISBN 0 340 79549 2

Typeset by Avon Dataset Ltd, Bidford-on-Avon, Warks

Printed and bound in Great Britain by
Clays Ltd, St Ives plc

Hodder Children's Books
a division of Hodder Headline Limited
338 Euston Road
London NW1 3BH

Also in the Nine Lives Series

Ginger, Nutmeg and Clove
Emerald, Amber and Jet
Daisy, Buttercup and Weed

The Return of Ginger, Nutmeg and Clove
The Return of Emerald, Amber and Jet

To Johnson,
a black-and-white prince among cats.

Nine Lives

Bracken is a large tortoiseshell cat who lives with the Bradman family on Liberty Street. Bracken lives a comfortable life, and spends much of her time snoozing away in her basket in the Bradmans' house.

Mr Bradman – Dad – used to be a lawyer, but he gave up this career for his real passion – gardening. He found Bracken abandoned in a skip two years ago when she was just a tiny kitten.

Mrs Bradman – Mum – is a bank manager. Unlike Mr Bradman, she loves her indoor office job.

Elsie Jennings – or Gran – is Mrs Bradman's mum. She lives a few doors away on Liberty Street. She may be over sixty-five, but Elsie has loads of get-up-and-go and enjoys being with children. That's why she loves her job as the local lollipop lady!

Tom Bradman is thirteen years old, and has an early morning job as a paperboy. He and his younger sister, Ellie, love animals. They always make a big fuss of Bracken and their six-year-old Golden Retriever, Lottie.

Ellie Bradman is ten years old. She's always coming up with brilliant plans and ideas – which is just as well, because earlier this year Bracken had her first litter. She became the proud mum of nine assorted bundles of fur . . .

* * *

Nine kittens; nine very different lives. The Bradmans knew they couldn't keep the kittens but they made sure that all nine went to the very best homes – homes to suit each, very special personality . . .

Daisy

1

"Miaow! Let me out of here!" Daisy wailed as she felt the car come to a stop. She pushed at the side of the cat-carrier with her front paw. It felt as if they had been driving for hours.

"Hooray! We're in Wales!" cried Mel, who was sitting on the back seat of the car next to Daisy's carrier. Daisy heard the door open and felt herself being lifted out of the car.

She heard Mel puffing under the weight of the cat-carrier as she walked along a stone path and then climbed some stairs.

At last, Mel put the carrier down on the floor and opened the lid. Daylight poured in, making Daisy blink. She jumped out of the carrier and stretched her back. "Thank goodness I'm out of there," she miaowed.

"Mum! I've let Daisy out!" called Mel. "Are you sure all the doors and windows are closed?"

"Yes," came Mrs Barnett's voice from downstairs. "But watch that she doesn't slip through the front door when Dad comes in."

"OK," said Mel. "I'll keep her in my room for a while." She went over to the door and closed it. "We don't want you getting lost, Daisy," she said.

"I don't want to get lost either," miaowed Daisy. She looked around the unfamiliar room. It was much smaller than Mel's bedroom at home. *I wonder what it's like outside*, thought Daisy. She jumped up onto the window sill. "Look at all that lovely grass!" she purred, staring out at a green field which stretched far into the distance. "I think I like Wales."

The Barnett family had come to North Wales on holiday. They were staying in a small cottage in the countryside. Mel hadn't wanted to leave Daisy in a cattery at home. She was worried that the little kitten would miss her too much. So Mr and Mrs Barnett had agreed to let Daisy come on holiday too, as long as Mel took good care of her.

Daisy gazed longingly outside. *I wish I could play out there*, she thought.

The field looked very tempting. Daisy could see butterflies dancing in the sunshine and birds flying from tree to tree. It would be so exciting to creep up on them. Daisy loved trying to catch birds in Mel's garden at home.

"I bet you'd like to be out there," said Mel, looking out of the window with Daisy. "Especially after that long journey in the car."

"It wasn't much fun," Daisy miaowed. "But it was better than being left behind."

Out of the corner of her eye, she spotted something moving in the field. "Look, Mel! What's that?" she miaowed.

A strange animal appeared from behind the hedge. It had a pale, shaggy coat, and it wasn't nearly as clean as Daisy. *It looks very grubby*, she thought. *What kind of animal lets itself get so dirty?* Daisy was proud of her thick, white coat. She always kept it very clean.

"Look, Daisy," said Mel. "There's a sheep. Can you see it?"

"I can see *lots* of sheep!" miaowed Daisy as a big flock of shaggy animals suddenly appeared from behind the hedge. "And they don't look very happy."

The sheep bustled across the field. They huddled together and made a loud bleating noise. They looked nervous and in a hurry.

"What's going on?" miaowed Daisy.

She soon found out. A black and white dog crept into the field. He slunk along behind the sheep, keeping low to the ground.

"And there's a sheepdog," said Mel. "Isn't he beautiful!"

The dog dropped to the ground and stared at the sheep. Daisy didn't think he looked beautiful at all. *He looks very fierce*! *I don't like the way he's glaring at the sheep*! she thought.

The sheep had stopped a little way ahead of the dog. They looked back anxiously at him. *It looks like he's stalking those sheep*, thought Daisy. She knew all about stalking. It was one of her favourite games. She often stalked birds and insects in Mel's garden.

Suddenly, Daisy heard a high-pitched whistle. The dog leaped to its feet. He ran quickly to one side of the sheep then flopped to the ground again. There was another shrill whistle. This time, the dog leaped up and ran straight towards the sheep, chasing them right across the field and out of sight.

Daisy felt sorry for the sheep. She wondered what would have happened if she'd been out in the field. Her tail bristled as she imagined what it would be like to be chased by the dog. *I'm glad I'm not there now. And I'm glad I'm not one of those sheep*, she thought.

"Don't worry about that collie dog," said Mel, noticing Daisy's fluffed-out tail. "He won't hurt you. He's just herding the sheep."

A man carrying a stick came into the field. He strode briskly after the dog, whistling loudly.

"There's the shepherd," said Mel, smoothing Daisy's puffed-up tail.

"Will he catch the dog before it catches the sheep?" miaowed Daisy anxiously as the man followed the dog out of sight. She wondered if the dog would get into trouble for chasing the sheep.

Mel picked up Daisy. "Let's go downstairs to tell Mum and Dad what we've just seen," she said, opening the bedroom door.

Daisy looked eagerly around her as Mel carried her out onto the narrow landing. At the top of the stairs, Daisy struggled to get down. She'd been cooped up long enough. She couldn't wait any longer to explore her new surroundings.

"No, Daisy. You can't get down yet," said Mel. She held onto her more tightly.

Daisy wriggled in Mel's arms.

"You're like a slippery eel," laughed Mel, trying to keep a firm hold of the kitten.

But Daisy was determined. "I'm going exploring!" she miaowed. With a mighty twist, she sprang out of Mel's arms.

"Watch out!" shouted Mel as Daisy streaked down the stairs. "Daisy's loose!"

Mel charged after the white kitten. The stairs creaked loudly as she ran. "Mum!" she yelled. "Make sure the front door's closed!"

Mrs Barnett appeared at the bottom of the stairs. "What a din! Calm down, Mel," she said. "Everything is shut. Daisy's quite safe." She picked up Daisy who was standing on the bottom step.

"Sorry, Mum," said Mel. "I was worried she'd escape."

"I won't escape," miaowed Daisy. "But I *do* want to go outside." Now that the sheepdog had gone, she felt sure it was safe to play in the field.

"Daisy will have to go out sometime," said Mrs Barnett. "So the sooner she feels at home here, the better." She turned and walked across the small living-room. "Let's give her something to eat. That'll help her to know she belongs here."

"I *know* I belong here," purred Daisy, "because you're all here too. But I don't mind having a snack. I'm starving!"

Mrs Barnett went into the tiny kitchen. She took a tin of cat food out of a cardboard box. "Here, Mel," she said, handing her the tin. "Give Daisy some of this."

Mel spooned some food into a bowl and put it on the floor in front of Daisy.

Daisy wolfed down the food then set about exploring the cottage. The living-room was full of interesting nooks and crannies. She poked her paw into a crack in the wall next to the fireplace. *I wonder what's in here?* she thought.

Daisy groped around until she felt something wriggling. She tried to catch it, but it slipped between her claws. Then something fell out of the crack. It was a big black beetle.

Daisy jumped back. The beetle scuttled

across the floor. Daisy waited until it was almost on the other side of the room before she ran after it and pounced. "Caught you!" she miaowed.

The beetle was trapped under her front paw. Daisy could feel it wriggling. She lifted her paw slowly. The beetle lay on its back. Its tiny legs waved wildly in the air as it tried to turn itself over.

Daisy gave it a prod. The beetle grabbed onto the fur of her paw. "Let go!" Daisy

miaowed, as she felt its prickly little claws hooking into her. She flicked her paw. The beetle shot across the room to the stairs.

In a flash, Daisy leaped after it. But this time, the beetle won. It scuttled into a narrow crack in the old wooden stairs and vanished.

Daisy decided not to waste any more time on the sneaky beetle. She wanted to explore the bedrooms. She bounded up the stairs which squeaked noisily beneath her.

"I didn't know one little kitten could make such a racket!" laughed Mel, who was watching Daisy from the bottom of the stairs.

"I can make even more noise than that," miaowed Daisy. She hurtled back down the stairs and bounded into the living-room. She was about to race up the stairs again when she heard a loud barking.

Wruff! *Wruff*! It sounded very close – as if a dog was in the living-room!

Daisy froze.

Wruff, wruff, wruff! The dog sounded very excited.

It must be that sheepdog again, thought Daisy

nervously. *What if it's coming after* me *now*?

She hunched herself up and flattened her ears. "Wherever you are, dog, don't come anywhere near me!" she hissed.

"You sound very fierce," said Mel.

"Do I?" miaowed Daisy, proudly. She hissed again – this time, more loudly.

When Daisy had first come to live with Mel and her parents, she couldn't purr or miaow. She had been the quietest of all Bracken's kittens. But one day, after she'd been with the Barnetts for about two months, she found herself in a situation where she *had* to make a noise.

Mel had been ill. She had fainted while she was playing with Daisy in her bedroom. Daisy alerted Mrs Barnett by miaowing loudly for the first time ever. Mrs Barnett took Mel to hospital, where she was treated and soon got better.

Everyone had been very pleased with Daisy for raising the alarm. Since then, she had really enjoyed using her voice and discovering all the different sounds she could make.

"*Wruff*!" barked the dog again.

"Go away!" hissed Daisy. She stood up and arched her back. If the dog was watching her, she needed to look very threatening.

Mel went over to the window. "I wonder where that dog is?" she said.

The barking continued.

"It's the sheepdog come to get me," miaowed Daisy.

"I think it's next door," said Mrs Barnett, coming in from the kitchen with a tray of tea.

"That's too close," hissed Daisy.

Mel glanced down at her. "Don't worry," she told the scared kitten. "You can put your fur down. The dog's not going to bother you."

But Daisy wasn't so sure. She couldn't help remembering how the collie dog had chased the poor sheep in the field. She was sure he had come back to chase her too. She was going to have to be extra careful when she went outdoors!

2

"I think you can take Daisy outside now," Mrs Barnett told Mel later that afternoon. "The front garden has a wall round it so she'll be quite safe there."

"Great!" miaowed Daisy, running towards the front door. At last, she was going to be able to explore outside.

The dog had stopped barking ages ago. Daisy had almost forgotten about him. She was only interested in what she would find outside.

Daisy padded happily about the small garden. She hunted amongst the shrubs and flowerbeds, disturbing grasshoppers and caterpillars.

"Catch this, Daisy," said Mel, rolling a small rubber ball towards her.

"That's easy!" miaowed Daisy. She stuck out her front paw. The ball bumped into her then bounced off down the path.

Daisy scampered after it. The ball rolled under the gate and out into the lane.

"Don't go through the gate!" called Mel.

"I won't," miaowed Daisy, peering between the bars. And then she froze. Charging straight towards her at full speed was a black-and-white dog!

Daisy tried to run, but her legs wouldn't move. She was rooted to the spot with fear. "Help!" she miaowed. "That sheepdog has come to chase me too!"

The dog was almost at the gate. Daisy could see his sharp teeth. Daisy hissed and fluffed up her fur. "Go away!" she spat.

The dog yapped excitedly then stopped in his tracks. He panted heavily but didn't come any closer.

Mel ran to Daisy and picked her up. "It's OK. He can't get through the gate," she said soothingly.

A young boy appeared behind the dog. "Hi," he said. "I'm Joe. I'm staying next door. And this is my spaniel, Patch."

Hearing his name, the spaniel gave another excited yap, then spun round and jumped up at Joe.

Spaniel? thought Daisy. *That means Patch isn't the sheepdog. Mel said that was a collie. I'll have to watch out for* two *dogs now!*

"I *thought* there must be a dog next door," said Mel. "We heard him barking earlier." She hugged Daisy. "He's just given my kitten a big fright."

"Sorry," said Joe. He held Patch's collar so that the dog couldn't jump up any more. "He ran off before I could press the button that stops his lead from getting longer." Joe showed the lead to Mel. "It's called an extendable lead. You can make it as long or as short as you like."

"That's a brilliant idea," said Mel. "It means the dog can run around, and you can make sure he doesn't go too far."

Joe nodded. "Patch is still only a puppy," he said. "That's why I have to keep him on a lead. Otherwise he might run off and get lost."

"I'm worried that Daisy might run off," said Mel.

Daisy rubbed her head against Mel's arms. "I keep telling you I won't," she miaowed. "Especially when there are dogs around. It's much safer staying with you."

Mel stroked Daisy's neck. "I wish we had a lead for you," she grinned. "Then you could go for lovely walks in the countryside – just like a dog."

"I don't want to be like a dog," miaowed Daisy. "But I *do* want to go exploring."

"I think we've got a spare lead," said Joe. "My mum will probably lend it to you if you ask her." He let go of the spaniel's collar. "Come on, Patch," he said. "Let's go down to the river."

After Joe and Patch had run off down the lane, Mel put Daisy on the grass. "I think we should try *you* out on a lead," she said.

"Try who on a lead?" asked Mrs Barnett. She had come into the garden and was unfolding a deckchair.

Mel told her mum about meeting Patch, and that Joe had offered to lend her a lead. "Will you come next door with me to ask if we can borrow one for Daisy?" she asked.

Mrs Barnett frowned. "I'm not sure it's a very good idea to put Daisy on a lead," she said. "Cats don't usually like being tied to one place."

"Please!" miaowed Daisy. "I'd love to go for a walk with Mel."

"Please!" begged Mel. "Let's just give it a try."

Mrs Barnett shrugged her shoulders. "All right. I suppose there's no harm in trying," she said. "Come on, then. Let's go next door."

Joe's mum was very helpful. She hunted about in a box full of dog things. "Here it is," she said at last, pulling out a long lightweight chain. "I knew we had a spare lead in here somewhere."

Mel clipped the chain onto Daisy's collar then put her on the floor. "How does that feel?" she asked.

"Fine," purred Daisy. "Let's go for a walk." Now that Daisy knew they were going out, she was very impatient to go and start exploring.

Mel walked around the room with Daisy trotting behind her. Daisy wasn't sure that she liked the feel of the chain pulling on her collar but she didn't want to complain. If it meant she could explore new places, then she'd put up with it.

Mel was delighted. "I think it's going to work! Thank you very much," she said to Joe's mum. "I think I'll take Daisy for her very first walk right now!"

Daisy felt a bit nervous as they started off down the lane. They were going in the same direction that Patch and Joe had gone. *I hope that dog's far away by now*, she thought. *I don't want to meet him again.* But she soon forgot her fears, as she padded along next to Mel. There were so many other things to think about.

The hedges on both sides of the lane were full of interesting noises and movements. Daisy didn't want to miss a thing so her senses were on full alert. She could hear mysterious scuttling sounds. She could also smell strange, new scents. Her eyes darted from side to side, fixing on anything that moved.

A small bird burst out of the hedge. It swooped right across Daisy's path and dived into a bush on the other side of the lane. Daisy took off after it. For a moment she forgot that she was attached to Mel by the chain.

"Careful, Daisy," shouted Mel, stumbling after her. Daisy heard a loud *Ouch*! as Mel crashed into the prickly bush.

Daisy hardly noticed Mel's cries. She was too busy looking for the bird. She scrambled up the narrow trunk inside the bush. *It must be in here somewhere*, she told herself.

Before Daisy could find out, Mel grabbed her and pulled her out of the bush. "Naughty kitten!" said Mel, putting her back on the path. "You're not supposed to go charging off like that. Now walk nicely next to me."

Daisy tried her best to be good. For a few minutes, she kept close to Mel. But the new smells on the path were very tempting. She just had to follow them. Before long, she was darting all over the lane.

"I give up!" laughed Mel, who was running helter-skelter behind her. "I'll just have to let *you* take *me* for a walk!"

"Great!" purred Daisy. "Now we'll *really* have fun." Her nose picked up a strong new scent. "Let's follow this one," she miaowed.

The smell zigzagged along the path then veered off to the side. "This way," Daisy miaowed, pulling Mel across the lane.

The scent disappeared at the bottom of a

tree. Daisy sniffed around until she caught a whiff of it again. *The trail goes up the tree*, she told herself. She sat and stared up into the branches.

"That's enough, Daisy," said Mel impatiently. "Let's go down to the river." She gave the chain a light tug. "It's your turn to follow me now."

Daisy stood up. She took one step then stopped and sniffed the air. She could smell something else. *I know that scent*, she said to herself. *I smelled it not long ago.*

The hair on her back stood up in a ridge as the scent grew stronger. Something about it made Daisy feel anxious. *It's coming towards us*, she realised. *And it definitely smells of danger*! Then all of a sudden, Daisy remembered where she'd smelled it. "It's Patch!" she miaowed. "He's coming back!"

She tried to run up the tree but couldn't move. Mel was holding the chain too tightly.

"Let me go!" Daisy howled.

At that moment, a loud barking broke out. It drowned Daisy's voice. "Mel!" she miaowed. "We have to run!" Her voice sounded even more feeble because, along with the barking, came the sound of galloping feet.

Before Mel and Daisy could run away, Patch appeared. He came hurtling round a bend in the lane and ran straight towards them.

"Joe should press the button on his lead!" cried Mel. "He must stop him!"

Daisy could see the dog's long black ears flapping up and down as he ran. She also saw something else – Patch was not attached to his lead and there was no sign of Joe! Daisy was afraid they were in terrible danger. Patch could *not* be stopped!

"Help!" miaowed Daisy.

Patch was now so close that Daisy could hear him panting. "You're *not* catching me!" she hissed. She tugged at the chain with all her might. She jerked it out of Mel's hands. In an instant, Daisy had scrambled up the tree.

It wasn't a moment too soon. Patch leaped

at the trunk, missing Daisy's tail by a whisker.

"*Mrreeooww*," wailed Daisy. "Someone come quickly!"

She looked down helplessly. Mel was still on the ground. She'd had no time to climb the tree to safety. Now Mel was all alone with the excited dog.

3

"Leave Mel alone!" hissed Daisy. She flattened her ears and howled as loudly as she could.

Patch ignored her. He bounced around Mel's feet, whining and yapping, and licked her knees.

He's going to eat Mel! Daisy's eyes were wide with fear. If only someone would come quickly. Then Mel would be rescued.

Someone did arrive. It was Joe. He came running round the bend and up the lane. "Patch!" he called. "Here, boy." He sounded very out of breath.

When he saw Patch, Joe slowed down. "Phew! I thought I'd lost him," he said when he reached Mel. "Somehow, he just slipped right out of his collar." He showed Mel the collar dangling at the end of the lead. "Thanks for stopping him."

Mel looked confused. "I didn't," she said. "Patch came charging at us. I thought he was going to attack me."

Joe laughed. "Patch isn't vicious. He's just very friendly."

"I know that now," grinned Mel. "At first I thought he wanted to bite my legs but then he just licked them!" She looked up at Daisy who was still clinging tightly to a branch. "Poor Daisy. She's had another big shock – just when she was having a lot of fun on her lead."

"I don't think Patch wanted to hurt her either," said Joe. He put the collar around

Patch's neck and buckled it tightly. "You see, his best friend is my gran's cat. They always play together when we visit Gran," he said. Joe slipped his hand under the collar to make sure it wasn't too tight.

"Well I'm not going to play with Patch," miaowed Daisy. "Even if he is friendly."

Mel began to coax her out of the tree. "Come on, Daisy," she said, standing on tiptoes trying to reach her. "Patch isn't going to attack you."

Daisy wriggled backwards, out of Mel's reach. "Tell him to go away," she mewed.

"Do you want me to climb up and get her?" asked Joe.

"Don't you dare!" miaowed Daisy. "You're not touching me. Not while that dog is with you. I'll come down by myself." She began to edge her way along the branch.

"You don't need to, Joe," said Mel. "I think she's going to come down on her own after all."

Daisy reached the trunk. She hooked her

claws into the bark then scrambled down backwards.

"Are you sure Patch won't hurt her?" asked Mel, grabbing Daisy as soon as she landed on the ground. Daisy snuggled into her arms and scowled at the dog.

Joe held on to Patch firmly. "I promise he won't," he said.

The spaniel trembled and whined with excitement.

Daisy thought he was just waiting for a chance to get free again. "Well *I'm* not sure!" she mewed. "Take him away!"

Joe didn't take Patch away. Instead, he led the puppy over to Mel and Daisy. "Make friends with the kitten," he said to Patch.

Daisy didn't like that idea one little bit! Especially when Patch jumped up and sniffed her.

"Ugh!" she hissed, shrinking back against Mel. Patch's damp nose blew puffs of warm, doggy air all over her fur. "Stop that!"

Patch stopped sniffing, but then he did something even worse. He began to lick

Daisy's face! In big swipes, his long, pink tongue swept back and forth, wetting her from ear to ear.

Daisy had had enough. She narrowed her eyes and growled softly. Patch took no notice of her. He continued licking. Angrily, Daisy opened her mouth wide and pulled her lips back so that he could see her sharp teeth. "I said *stop that*!" she hissed fiercely. Then she lashed out with a paw and batted him across the nose.

Patch sprang back in surprise. He whimpered softly and frowned at Daisy. She glared proudly at him. *He's not that brave after all*, she thought.

"I don't think Daisy wants to be friends with a dog," chuckled Joe.

"No," agreed Mel. "Even though she's been for a walk on a lead!" She kissed Daisy on the top of her head. "You're not at all like a dog, are you?"

"Definitely not!" miaowed Daisy.

The next day was hot and sunny. Mel and her parents were packing a picnic. They planned to spend the afternoon in the field behind the cottage.

I hope they're taking me too, thought Daisy. "Please can I go with you?" she mewed, twisting herself in and out of Mrs Barnett's legs. Even though she had seen the sheepdog in the field the day before, Daisy was still very keen to go exploring there. She had already come face-to-face with a bouncy puppy, so she felt much braver about meeting other dogs.

Mrs Barnett put the picnic basket on the floor next to the door while she went to fetch her book.

"I'll get in there. Then they'll *have* to take me," mewed Daisy. She jumped into the basket. There wasn't much room but she managed to squeeze herself into a gap next to the flask of tea.

Mr Barnett bent down to pick up the picnic basket. At first he didn't see Daisy. "Are we all ready?" he asked.

"Yes," miaowed Daisy. "Let's go."

Mr Barnett stared into the basket. "Daisy!" he laughed when he saw her. "What do you think you're doing?"

"Going for a picnic in the field with you," she miaowed.

"I think she wants to come with us," grinned Mel. "I'll get the chain."

Mr and Mrs Barnett looked at each other and shook their heads.

"She'll get so used to walking on a lead, you'll be able to take her shopping when we get home, Mel," laughed Mrs Barnett.

"That would be nice," purred Daisy. "Jet would be surprised to see me on a lead." Jet was one of her brothers. He lived at the corner shop in Liberty Street, not far from the Barnetts' house.

The field was even more exciting than Daisy had imagined. There were creatures everywhere! Beetles stumbled through the grass, and ants scurried busily to and fro. Bumble bees hovered in the air then suddenly buzzed away to find another flower. Butterflies floated in the gentle breeze and grasshoppers leaped through the tall grass.

Daisy's head spun round. There was so much to see. Soon she felt dizzy from trying to watch everything that was going on around her.

A dragonfly burst out from the grass in front of her. It fluttered away across the field. Daisy tried to chase it but the chain held her back. She tugged at it, trying to pull it out of Mel's hands – just as she had done the day before in the lane.

"All right, Daisy," said Mel. "I'll let you

off – as long as you don't go too far." She unclipped the lead.

"That's much better," miaowed Daisy. She lay on her tummy in the grass and watched a hairy caterpillar crawling along. It hunched itself up then stretched itself out then hunched itself up again. Each time it stretched out flat on the ground, it moved a little way forwards.

"I'll try that," mewed Daisy. She arched her back then pushed out her front legs. "I did it!" she purred, feeling herself move forward.

Daisy crawled after the caterpillar for a few more minutes. When she looked back over her shoulder, she realised that she had moved quite far away from Mel and her parents. They were lying in the grass dozing after their picnic lunch.

Suddenly, Mel sat up and looked around. "Daisy!" she called. "Where are you?"

"Over here," miaowed Daisy, jumping up and bounding through the grass to her.

"Phew! For a minute I thought you'd got

lost," sighed Mel. "Don't go so far away!" She lay down again on the blanket.

"I didn't mean to," mewed Daisy. She curled up next to Mel and purred. "I'll have a nap with you."

Daisy's nap was no more than a catnap. She shut her eyes. A second later, she opened them again. Something was buzzing above her head. It was a bee.

Daisy swiped at it with a paw.

"Careful," warned Mel, rolling onto her stomach. "It'll sting you." She rested her chin on her hands and watched Daisy.

"I don't want to catch it," miaowed Daisy. "Just chase it."

The bee spiralled upwards. Daisy was on her feet in a flash. She sprang off the ground and launched herself through the air. The bee soared higher. Daisy landed on the ground but leaped up again immediately. This time, she batted the bee with her paw. It dived to one side then flew jerkily away.

Daisy raced after it. *This is such fun*! she thought to herself. *What a lovely place*! Then she suddenly remembered what had happened to the sheep in this field. What if that collie dog came back?

Daisy whirled round. Mel now seemed very far away. Too far for Daisy to feel safe if the sheepdog appeared. With a burst of speed, Daisy raced back to Mel.

"Don't you think you ought to clip the chain onto Daisy's collar again, Mel?" said Mrs Barnett, seeing Daisy rushing back to them. "She keeps wandering off."

"I'm all right, really!" miaowed Daisy. She snuggled up next to Mel. "I don't want to go too far away on my own. It's much safer here with you."

Mel rolled over. "But Daisy always comes back, Mum," she said. "And I don't think cats need leads."

"That's right," purred Daisy. "We're not dogs."

Mel sat up. "And anyway, I've got a special chain for Daisy," she went on.

"A special chain for me?" miaowed Daisy, jumping onto Mel's lap. She spotted a pile of pretty white-and-yellow flowers lying beside Mel. Daisy leaned across and sniffed at them.

"Just a minute, Daisy," chuckled Mel. She picked up the flowers. Daisy noticed that they were all linked together. They formed a little circle in the palm of Mel's hand.

"I've been making this for you, Daisy," said Mel.

Daisy reached out and gently tapped the flowers with one paw. "They're very pretty," she mewed.

Mel smiled. "I think this will suit you much better than the dog's chain," she said, carefully placing the flowers round Daisy's neck. "It's your very own daisy chain!"

Buttercup

1

"Miaow! What's that?" Buttercup woke with a jolt. She sprang to her feet, arching her back and fluffing out her tail. Who was disturbing her afternoon nap in the garden?

A tumbling bundle of black, white and ginger fur crashed into her. Buttercup was bowled off her feet. She landed against the trunk of the apple tree.

"Sorry, Buttercup! We didn't see you

sleeping there," came a friendly miaow.

"Hello, Thin! Hello, Basil! What are you doing?" Buttercup miaowed as she recognised her two friends. "I thought you were something fierce attacking me."

"We were just chasing that paper cup," replied Thin. He was a skinny black-and-white cat, and Basil was a large ginger tom with a torn ear.

Buttercup scrambled to her feet and looked around. "What paper cup?" she asked.

Basil dabbed his paw at some white paper lying on the grass beneath Buttercup's paws. "This one!" he miaowed.

"That's not a cup. It's a piece of paper," miaowed Buttercup, sniffing at it.

"It is *now*," mewed Thin sadly. "But it *was* a cup – until you fell on it and squashed it." He hooked the paper with his claws and flicked it into the air. The flattened cup fell to the ground. "Pity!" he sighed. "I don't think it'll work any more. And it was a really good toy."

"Toy?" miaowed Buttercup. It didn't look

much like a toy to her – more like a piece of rubbish. The Chapmans, who owned the house where Buttercup lived, would have thrown it away.

The Chapmans were a big, noisy family. Apart from Mr and Mrs Chapman, there were five children – Freddie, Clare, Jim, Gilly and baby Lee, as well as Gran and Grandad who lived in the basement flat. Buttercup loved living with them. There was always someone to play with.

Basil prodded the paper cup again. "Oh dear!" he miaowed. "Thin's right. It was such a good toy! The wind blew it all the way into your garden."

Thin flopped down onto the lawn. "We were pretending the cup was a white bird," he purred, rolling from side to side in the dust. "When it blew behind the tree, we pounced. And that's when we landed on you," he explained. Thin sat up and shook himself. A cloud of dust flew off him. "You see, it's really hard to spot you in the shade, Buttercup."

Buttercup's coat was known as tortie. Her fur had all sorts of colours in it – marmalade, tabby, tortoiseshell, black, brown and white. Sometimes, when she lay under a tree, she could hardly be seen because she blended so well with the dappled shade.

Buttercup looked sadly at her friends. "Sorry I spoiled your fun," she miaowed.

"It's not your fault," answered Thin. "We knocked you over."

"Anyway, we can always find something else to play with," miaowed Basil cheerfully. A leaf drifted down from the tree. As quick as lightning, he leaped up and grabbed it with his big ginger front paws. "See," he miaowed, landing lightly on the ground. "Leaves are lots of fun too." Basil gripped the stalk between his teeth and shook the leaf fiercely.

"They're great toys!" agreed Thin. He crouched on the grass and looked up into the tree. As soon as he spotted another leaf floating down, he threw himself into the air to catch it.

Buttercup sat beneath the apple tree and

watched her friends happily chasing leaves.

Basil and Thin didn't belong to anyone. They often came to play with Buttercup in her garden. Once, they'd brought along some of their friends to play with all the Chapmans so that Buttercup could get some rest. Sometimes Buttercup couldn't get any peace and quiet because everyone in the family wanted to play with her.

"Hey! This is exciting," growled Basil. A leaf was trapped in his paws and he was ripping it up with his sharp teeth.

"Is it?" miaowed Buttercup. It didn't look very exciting to her. She was used to the more interesting toys that the children gave to her.

"Yes. Try it," miaowed Basil. "Look, there's one now."

Buttercup jumped up and clawed at a leaf wafting down towards her. Just as she touched it, a breeze blew it out of reach.

"I'll catch it," miaowed Thin, springing after it.

The leaf tumbled away then swirled upwards in the wind. It almost seemed alive. *I suppose you* could *pretend it's a bird or a butterfly*, thought Buttercup.

Thin stretched his scrawny black-and-white body and threw himself at the leaf again. With a quick swipe of his paw, he finally caught it. "Got you!" he growled, landing on all fours and pinning the leaf to the ground.

As the wind picked up, more leaves drifted around the garden. Basil and Thin darted after as many as they could. Buttercup joined in and caught a few. It was fun – but not nearly as much fun as chasing a ball.

After a while, they grew tired of the game. "What shall we play now?" asked Basil. He was sitting on a small pile of torn leaves. Buttercup thought it looked like he was in a nest.

"How about chase-my-tail?" miaowed Thin. He started whizzing round in a circle, trying to catch his tail in his mouth.

"You'll have to go faster," miaowed Basil. "Like this." And he began to spin round so quickly that Buttercup felt dizzy watching him. She decided to try the new game too. Twisting round, she made a grab for her tail. But the tip was just out of reach. She lunged at it again, but still it escaped her.

This is a silly game, she thought. She stopped and looked at Basil and Thin. They were twirling so fast that they had become blurs of orange and black and white. Buttercup began to feel sorry for her friends. *They've got no proper cat toys to play with*, she thought.

That's why they have to chase bits of rubbish and leaves, and even their own tails!

Finally the two cats stopped spinning. "It's no good," panted Thin. "I can't get anywhere near it!"

"Me neither," miaowed Basil, slumping to the ground.

"And *I* couldn't grab even one hair!" mewed Buttercup.

Basil had a new idea. "Let's look for another paper cup in the street!" he suggested, jumping to his paws.

"OK," miaowed Thin. He flicked his tail then glared at it over his shoulder. "I'll catch you one day," he growled at the white tip.

The three friends trotted across the lawn and jumped onto the garden wall. They walked along the top of the wall in single file, ready to pounce if they saw a paper cup on the ground below.

"There's one!" miaowed Thin suddenly. "Let's go." He dropped down onto the pavement.

Basil jumped down behind him. "Coming,

Buttercup?" he miaowed, glancing up at her.

Buttercup hesitated. She had had an idea. Basil and Thin didn't *have* to play with boring paper cups. She could make sure of that. "No," she miaowed. "I have to go back home now."

Basil looked disappointed. "Don't you want to play with us any more?"

"Of course I do. That's why I'm going home," Buttercup replied mysteriously. She jumped down from the wall into her garden.

Buttercup purred loudly to herself as she pushed open her cat-flap in the kitchen door. She could hardly wait to put her plan into action.

"Miaow?" she called loudly, padding into the house. "Does anyone want to play ball with me?"

In the hallway, Buttercup found baby Lee. He was sitting on the floor surrounded by all sorts of toys.

"Buttcup, Buttcup," Lee gurgled when he saw her. "Play car." He rolled a small metal car towards her.

Buttercup jumped out of the way of the car. It rolled past her and crashed into the skirting board.

"Crash!" yelled Lee happily. He grabbed a big plastic lorry and pushed it towards Buttercup.

"I don't want to play cars," mewed Buttercup, dodging the lorry. "I want to play ball." She prodded the heap of toys with her paw until she spotted what she was looking for. "Found it!" she miaowed, flicking a small transparent ball into the air.

The ball landed on the floor, bounced once, then rolled away. It made a tiny, jingling sound. *There's a bell in it*, thought Buttercup happily.

The ball bumped into the car and stopped.

"Crash!" shouted Lee again.

Buttercup scampered over to the ball. Now all she had to do was hide it from baby Lee.

"Push the car, Buttcup!" shouted the baby.

Here was her chance! Buttercup gave the little red car a hard push with one paw. It rolled towards Lee who squealed with delight. While the baby was watching the car, Buttercup pushed the jingling ball behind the sofa.

That's one *toy for Basil and Thin*, she told herself. *Four more to go*!

Buttercup spent the rest of the day collecting balls from the children. The next one was a white ping-pong ball. Nine-year-old Freddie was batting it against a wall in his bedroom. Buttercup waited until he missed the ball. She watched it roll under his bed.

"I'll pick it up later," Freddie said, and he sat down to play a computer game.

And I'll take it now, thought Buttercup. She flattened herself on the floor and squeezed her way under the bed. Then she nosed the ball out and patted it across the room and out of the door. Freddie was so busy playing his game that he didn't notice her taking the ball away.

At the top of the stairs, Buttercup tapped the ball lightly. It bounced down the stairs to the hallway. She scampered after it just in time to see it roll behind the sofa. *That was easy*! she thought.

It wasn't quite so easy to collect the third ball. Clare, who was seven, had a pretty sparkly pink ball. It was her favourite and she loved to watch Buttercup playing with it. But as soon as the game was over, Clare always put the ball on a shelf above her bed. Clare kept all her favourite things there.

Buttercup waited for Clare to come out of her room. Then, quietly, she sneaked in. *There it is*! She could see the pink ball on the shelf high above her. She jumped onto the bed and from there she leaped up onto the shelf.

As she landed, the shelf wobbled under her weight. Buttercup hung on with all her might. There was a loud creaking noise and she felt herself falling backwards. The shelf had come away from the wall!

Buttercup landed with a thud on the bed. All of Clare's special things came crashing down on top of her. The china ornaments clinked loudly as they landed.

"What's going on in there?" came Clare's voice from the landing.

Buttercup's heart began to pound. She could hear footsteps coming. Swiftly, Buttercup grabbed the pink ball in her mouth and tore out of the room. Behind her she heard Clare shout crossly, "Oh no! Look what Buttercup's done!"

Soon the sparkly ball was safely hidden behind the sofa. Buttercup went in search of the next one. Five-year-old Jim had a bouncy blue rubber ball. He often threw it for Buttercup and it would bounce high into the air. Buttercup loved to fling herself into the air after it.

She found the blue ball in a corner on the landing. With a tap she sent it bouncing down the stairs. But the more the ball bounced, the higher it flew. Soon it was hitting the ceiling! Then it hit a wall and bounced right across the hall into the living-room.

Jim was watching television in the living-room. The ball landed on the floor next to him, bounced high up one more time and landed on a chair. Buttercup ran into the room after the ball.

"I'll play ball with you later, Buttercup," said Jim. "I want to watch TV now."

"That's OK," miaowed Buttercup. She picked up the blue rubber ball in her mouth and trotted out to the hallway. She wasn't going to let it bounce away again!

The last ball belonged to four-year-old Gilly. It was a soft sponge tennis ball. Buttercup found it lying under the dining-room table. It was too big for her to carry in her mouth so she had to push it all the way to the hall. But the squashy yellow ball kept bumping into chairs and getting stuck behind things.

Then Gilly spotted Buttercup. "I want to play too," she said. Gilly picked up the ball and ran into the dining-room, calling, "Catch me, Buttercup."

Buttercup went back into the dining-room. Gilly rolled the ball towards her. Buttercup started pushing it towards the door again. But every time Buttercup pushed it as far as the door, Gilly would grab it and run back into the dining-room, laughing.

After a while, Gilly grew tired of the game and went to play outdoors. Buttercup was worn out. But at last she had the sponge ball.

She rolled it into the hallway and nudged it behind the sofa. Then, lying flat on the floor, she peeped at her little collection of balls. They were perfect! Basil and Thin would have a great time playing with them.

2

"Bye, Buttercup. See you later," said Freddie. It was early the next day. Freddie gave Buttercup a quick stroke before running out of the door.

"Did you leave any food out for Buttercup?" called Mrs Chapman. "Remember, we won't be home till late this afternoon."

"Yes, Mum," Freddie called back. "Her dish is full."

That's good, thought Buttercup. *I'll be needing lots of food today.*

She sat in the hallway waiting for the family to leave. They were going to visit their cousins who lived in another town.

"Be a good kitten," said Mr Chapman, bending down to stroke her. "No clambering about on shelves!" He had just finished putting Clare's shelf back on the wall.

"I won't, I promise," miaowed Buttercup. She had better things to do!

The door closed behind Mr Chapman. Buttercup heard the key turn in the lock. A few minutes later, she heard the sound of the car pulling away.

"Hooray! Now I've got the whole house to myself," she miaowed. "Time for the big surprise. First, I'll have to find Basil and Thin."

Buttercup pushed open her cat-flap and ran out onto the pavement. She looked up and down the street but saw no sign of her friends. *I'll try the alley behind the shops*, she decided.

"Thin! Basil!" she called as she made her way along the narrow alley.

Just ahead of her, the back door of the fish shop burst open. "Shoo! Out of here! Scram!" shouted a woman. A streak of ginger shot out of the door and hid behind a dustbin. "I only wanted the leftovers," came a forlorn miaow.

"And don't come back!" said the angry woman, slamming the door.

"Basil!" miaowed Buttercup loudly. "Come out here!"

Basil peeped out from his hiding place. "Buttercup! What are you doing here?" he miaowed.

"I've come to fetch you," she replied. "I have a surprise for you."

"A surprise for me?" miaowed Basil.

"And for Thin," mewed Buttercup. "Do you know where he is?"

Basil scratched his ear. "Well, he's not in the fish shop. That's for sure. That angry woman would have thrown him out too," he miaowed. "I thought she would be pleased if I ate the bits she had dropped on the floor."

"Don't worry about that woman," miaowed Buttercup. "Let's find Thin. Then you'll get your surprise."

"That sounds like a good idea," said Basil. "What is it?"

"I'm not telling you yet," answered Buttercup. "Otherwise it won't be a surprise any more."

The two friends set off down the alley. They checked behind dustbins and inside cardboard boxes.

"Thin doesn't usually come down here," remembered Basil, when they reached the end of the alley. "He prefers open, sunny places." He looked up. "Like roofs."

Buttercup looked up too. "You're right," she miaowed. "And there he is!"

A black-and-white face was peering down at them over the edge of the gutter. "Hello, you two," miaowed Thin. "What are you doing in the alley? Hunting mice?"

"No," answered Basil. "Getting chased by the fish woman!"

Thin sighed. "Not again!" he miaowed.

"When are you going to learn that you won't get anything to eat from her?"

"I know," miaowed Basil. "But I was hungry. I just can't resist the smell coming from her shop."

"I've got food for you if you're hungry," offered Buttercup.

"Is that the surprise?" asked Basil eagerly.

"No. It's better than that," Buttercup told him.

Thin pricked up his ears. "Surprise? And it's better than food! What is it?" he asked.

"You'll see," miaowed Buttercup. "But you have to come with me."

Thin quickly clambered down a drainpipe. "I'm ready. Lead the way," he miaowed.

The three cats ran back to the Chapmans' house. Buttercup pushed the cat-flap open and her friends followed her into the hallway. "The surprise is behind this sofa," she told them.

Thin and Basil squeezed into the gap behind the sofa. "Wow!" miaowed Thin. "Look at these lovely balls." He backed out of the gap with the sparkly pink ball in his mouth. "Can we play with them?"

Buttercup purred. "Yes. That's what they're for," she mewed. She felt very pleased that her friends liked the surprise.

"Where did all these nice toys come from?" asked Basil, pushing the ping-pong ball out into the hall.

"The children," Buttercup told him. "I took a ball from each of them."

Thin's face fell. "So we can't really play with the balls," he miaowed sadly. "They're not ours."

"Yes, they are," miaowed Buttercup. "The children won't miss them. And anyway, nobody's at home today." She headed for the kitchen. "Come on. Let's have something to eat first."

"Good idea," purred Basil, trotting after her. "I'm really starving now."

Freddie had left plenty of food in Buttercup's dish.

"Hey!" miaowed Basil, sniffing the food. "Another surprise. Fish!"

"And it's better than the scraps on the floor in the fish shop," purred Thin, tucking hungrily into the food.

In no time at all, the bowl was empty. The three cats sat side by side and cleaned their whiskers and paws. Then Buttercup dashed back into the hall. "Playtime!" she miaowed.

Thin and Basil raced after her. "Let's take the balls outside," suggested Thin.

They each picked up one ball. Thin chose the ping-pong ball. He held it gently in his

mouth so that his teeth wouldn't make a hole in it and carried it into the garden. Basil took out the bouncy rubber ball and Buttercup carried Lee's jingling ball. Then they went back to collect the other two.

Thin had a few problems getting the sponge tennis ball through the cat-flap. It was too big to fit into his mouth and it bumped into the door when he tried to push it through. Then Basil managed to flick the ball through the flap with his strong front paws.

At last, the five balls lay in a heap on the lawn. Basil and Thin stared at them in delight for a few minutes. Then Basil bent down and sniffed at the ping-pong ball. It rolled off a little way.

"Hey, this ball moves on its own!" he miaowed excitedly. "It's alive!"

"No, it's not," miaowed Thin. He sniffed at the ball too. Again it rolled away. Basil and Thin padded over to it and sniffed at it together. This time, the ball rolled even further. "It *is* alive!" Basil insisted.

"It's not," miaowed Buttercup. "You're breathing on it. That's why it's moving! Watch." She breathed out hard. The ping-pong ball bounced away. Thin and Basil dashed after it, breathing out through their noses and making it whizz ahead of them. Buttercup thought they looked very funny!

"Try this one," she miaowed after a while. She tapped the ball with the bell inside. It jingled across the grass to Thin. He tapped it back. Basil pounced on it. The bell jingled loudly. "It sounds like it's talking to me," miaowed Basil.

Soon, they were playing with all the balls. Basil and Thin loved flicking the blue rubber ball into the air then chasing after it as it bounced all over the garden. Once it went right over the hedge into the garden next door. Buttercup scampered after it and brought it back.

Then the cats chased the sponge tennis ball. It was light and moved very quickly. But they soon learned not to dig their claws into it. If they did, they had to unhook them again.

Buttercup liked the sparkly ball best of all because it glinted and flashed in the sunshine. She thought it was the prettiest toy she had ever seen.

The day passed very quickly, and the cats really enjoyed playing with the balls. But Basil and Thin couldn't help worrying that the children would be sad when they found that their toys were missing.

"I don't think they'll mind," miaowed Buttercup.

Suddenly, Thin pricked up his ears. "What's that?" he asked.

Buttercup listened. There were voices coming from the house. "It's my family," she miaowed. "They've come home."

"Buttercup!" Mrs Chapman was calling her. "Where are you?"

"We've got to go!" miaowed Basil anxiously. "They'll be cross if they see us with all these toys."

Before Buttercup could say anything, Thin

and Basil were off! They leaped over the wall and disappeared silently.

"There you are!" said Mrs Chapman, coming out into the garden. "Have you been very lonely?"

"No," purred Buttercup. She rubbed herself against Mrs Chapman's legs. "I've had a lovely time."

"Hey! Look at this!" said Freddy. He and the other children had come outside to look for Buttercup. "How did all these balls get here?"

Buttercup wound herself around Mrs Chapman's legs. "I only borrowed them," she mewed innocently.

"How strange!" said Mrs Chapman. "There are five balls out here – each belonging to one of you. Did you bring them out, Gilly?"

Gilly shook her head.

"And look! Here's my best ball," said Clare, picking up the sparkly pink ball. "I've been searching all over for it." She looked at Buttercup who was peering around Mrs

Chapman's legs. "Maybe Buttercup brought them out here."

"Please don't be cross with me," Buttercup miaowed. "I was only trying to do something nice for my friends."

3

"Well, it's a bit of a mystery," laughed Mrs Chapman. "But it certainly looks as if Buttercup is the culprit. After all, she was the only one here all day."

"I wasn't," miaowed Buttercup. "Thin and Basil were here too."

"And I know for sure that the balls weren't in the garden this morning," went on Mrs Chapman, "because I came out to collect the washing before we left." She picked up Buttercup. "I wonder what you've been up to all day?" she said.

"Playing ball with Basil and Thin," purred Buttercup.

Mrs Chapman stroked her soft fur. "If only cats could talk to us," she said with a smile, putting Buttercup back on the ground, "then we'd be able to find out what's been going on here."

"I *am* talking to you," miaowed Buttercup. "And I *told* you what we've been doing."

The children picked up the balls and took them back to their bedrooms. Buttercup followed them indoors. She thought about how much Basil and Thin had enjoyed playing with real toys for a change. If only her friends could have kept the balls for ever. Now they would have to go back to playing with rubbish and leaves again.

Later, at supper, the family tried to work out the puzzle of the balls. Buttercup sat in her basket in the corner, listening to the conversation.

"But if it *was* Buttercup who took them out there," said Freddie, "how did she manage to take them all outside by herself?"

"I didn't," miaowed Buttercup from her basket. "Basil and Thin helped me."

"And even if she *did* take them out herself, why did she want so many?" asked Clare, frowning at Buttercup. "One ball is enough for a cat to play with."

"We played with *all* of them," purred Buttercup, remembering how much fun they'd had. "They're all so different and they do very different things." She jumped out of her basket and trotted over to the table. "I wish you'd let me have them back," she miaowed, winding herself in and out of everyone's legs. "They're the best toys in the world."

When Buttercup came to Mr Chapman's legs, he reached down and scratched her behind her ears. She pushed her head against his hand and purred loudly.

"So, little Buttercup," chuckled Mr Chapman. "You've been collecting pretty things, have you? You must be turning into a magpie!"

"What's a magpie?" asked Gilly, looking under the table at Buttercup.

"It's a bird that collects shiny things," said Mrs Chapman.

"But a cat can't change into a bird!" Gilly sounded very confused.

Mr Chapman laughed and explained that it was a joke. "But it *does* look as if Buttercup collected all those balls," he said. "She must have thought they were all pretty."

Freddie frowned. "They aren't *all* pretty. Especially my ping-pong ball. It's just plain white. I think it looks quite boring," he said.

"It's not boring at all," miaowed Buttercup. "We loved it!"

"My sparkly pink ball is pretty," said Clare. "If I was a cat, I think I'd like it the most."

"It *is* my favourite," miaowed Buttercup. "But we also liked the tinkling bell in Lee's ball, and the way Jim's ball bounced everywhere. Gilly's soft ball was lots of fun too." But the very best thing was being able to share the toys with her friends Thin and Basil.

"Oh well," said Mrs Chapman, getting up from the table. "I suppose we'll never get to the bottom of it. Buttercup must have wanted those balls for some reason."

"Wake up, Buttercup."

It was the next afternoon. Buttercup was fast asleep in her cosy basket. Freddie's voice made her stir. "Wake up, Buttercup," he said again, stroking her lightly down her back.

Buttercup uncurled her tail and stretched her legs. "I was having such a nice dream," she mewed as she opened her eyes. "I was playing with Basil and Thin in a garden full of balls."

Freddie was sitting on the floor next to her basket. He grinned at her. "Sorry to disturb you," he said. "But I don't think you'll mind waking up when you see what I have for you."

Buttercup was on her feet in an instant. "What is it?" she miaowed. She stood on the edge of her basket and pushed her head up towards Freddie. Her pink nose began to twitch as she caught the scent of something new.

Freddie laughed. "I think you're going to like it," he told her.

"What have you got?" miaowed Buttercup again. She saw that Freddie was holding one of his hands behind his back. Buttercup jumped onto his lap. Then she stood up with her front paws on his shoulder. She tried to see what he was hiding.

"OK, OK," laughed Freddie. "You can have it now." He brought his hand out from behind him and held it out in front of Buttercup. "What do you think of this?"

Buttercup stared in wonder. Freddie was holding the most beautiful ball she had ever seen. It was red, green and yellow and just the right size to be a good toy for cats. "Is it really for me?" she purred, too surprised to even sniff at it.

"Don't you want it?" smiled Freddie, moving his hand closer to her.

"Yes, please!" purred Buttercup. She

touched the ball with her nose. It smelled a bit like Jim's rubber ball. She dabbed at it with one paw. The ball rolled over in Freddie's hand. She patted it again. This time, it rolled right off Freddie's palm and bounced onto the floor.

Buttercup leaped off Freddie's lap after the ball. It hit the side of her basket then bounced through the air across the room. Buttercup could see flashes of red, green and yellow as she charged after it.

"I knew you'd like it," said Freddie.

Buttercup leaped up and caught the ball in the air. She landed with it between her front paws. There was a sharp squeak.

"What was that?" Buttercup miaowed, jumping back.

Freddie laughed loudly. "That's another surprise for you!" He came over to Buttercup and picked up the ball. "Listen to this," he said. He squeezed the ball in his hand. There was another loud squeak. "Isn't that great?" grinned Freddie. He rolled the ball across the floor.

Buttercup ran after it and pounced. *Squeak, squeak*, went the ball as Buttercup landed on it. She looked up at Freddie and blinked slowly. "Thank you," she purred. "It's the best ball in the whole world."

Later, when Freddie was playing with his computer game, Buttercup picked up her new ball in her mouth and trotted outside. She looked around for a safe hiding place.

There was a small hole at the bottom of the garden wall. Making sure that no one was watching her, Buttercup carefully put her ball in the hole. Then she jumped up onto the wall and down onto the pavement on the other side.

She headed straight for the alley. "Basil!" she miaowed as she reached the entrance.

"Miaow!" came a muffled reply.

Buttercup stared into the shadows. The lid of a cardboard box flipped open. Two ginger ears appeared.

"Is that you, Basil?" miaowed Buttercup.

"Yes, it is," grunted Basil. He pushed his head out of the box and Buttercup saw immediately what he was doing. Sticking out of his mouth was a paper cup!

Just then, Thin popped out from behind a bin. "Found one," he called to Basil, flicking another crumpled paper cup in front of him.

Buttercup trotted over to her friends. "You don't need those," she miaowed.

"Yes, we do," mewed Thin. "We want to chase them."

"I have something much nicer for you to chase," miaowed Buttercup. "Come with me and I'll show you." She led the way back to her hidey hole in the garden wall.

When Basil and Thin saw the colourful ball, they looked sad. "We can't play with the children's toys again," miaowed Basil.

Thin agreed. "We'll stick to our paper cups."

"But we *can* play with it," insisted Buttercup. She gave the ball a shove with her front paw. It rolled across the lawn. She ran after it and pounced, making it squeak loudly.

"That's great!" miaowed Basil. "I'd love to do that."

"And you can," Buttercup told him. "Whenever you like. You see, it's my very own ball. Freddie gave it to me."

Basil and Thin looked delighted. Buttercup tapped the ball towards them. Basil pounced. *Squeeeeak*! Then Thin flicked it into the air. The ball bounced against the wall and flew across the garden in a flash of red, green and yellow.

All three cats bounded after the ball. Buttercup felt very happy. *I really like my new ball*, she thought. *And I think my friends like it much more than old paper cups*!

Weed

1

Weed looked out of the window. Her sister, Nutmeg, was trotting down the garden path. *She must be coming to play*, Weed thought. *I'll go out to meet her.*

Weed looked down from the window sill to the floor below. It was much too far for her to jump down. She would have to use the armchair – just as she did when she climbed up.

The armchair was near the window. Weed leaped onto it and hooked her claws into the soft back. She felt the chair wobble beneath her. Quickly, she jumped down to the seat then onto the floor. *Everything is always too high or too far*, she thought to herself as she padded towards the door.

Weed was very tiny. Her mother, Bracken, had given birth to nine kittens in the Bradmans' house in Liberty Street. Weed was the last one to be born. She was also the last one to go to a new home. A lot of people came to look at her, but no one wanted a small, scraggy kitten. No one, that is, except for Gran – Tom and Ellie Bradmans' grandmother. Gran had always had a soft spot for Weed and finally took her home to live with her.

Gran lived in a flat with a garden just down the road from the Bradmans. Her real name was Elsie Jennings and she was the local lollipop lady. She helped children to cross the busy main road as they went to and from school.

"Going out to play?" asked Gran as Weed trotted past her in the hallway.

"Yes," miaowed Weed. "Nutmeg's coming too." She jumped through the cat-flap and met Nutmeg on the path outside.

Weed loved playing with her big sister. Nutmeg was brave and very inquisitive. Weed wanted to be just like her.

Weed and Nutmeg greeted each other by touching noses. They sniffed at each other for a few moments then Weed asked, "What shall we do today?"

"Let's go hunting," suggested Nutmeg.

"OK," miaowed Weed eagerly. "We can chase butterflies in the garden." She ran towards a flowerbed.

Nutmeg followed her and they hid amongst the flowers. They waited patiently for something to chase. At last a pretty blue butterfly flitted past Weed. She swiped at it with her paw. But the butterfly was just beyond her reach.

"If my legs were a bit longer, I would have caught it," she mewed sadly.

The kittens lay very still in the flowerbed but nothing else came their way. Soon, Weed grew bored with waiting. "Let's go somewhere else," she miaowed, standing up and stretching her neck so that she could see over the flowers.

Nutmeg stood up too. "Let's try over there," she suggested, glancing over her shoulder.

Weed had to push her way past the flowers to see where Nutmeg was looking. "Do you mean over there by the garden wall?" she asked.

"Yes," miaowed Nutmeg. "We can sit on the wall and look for insects in the shrubs below. When we see something, we can drop down onto it."

"Good idea!" miaowed Weed. "Let's go!"

They scampered across the lawn. When they reached the wall, Nutmeg leaped up onto it with ease. "Come on!" she miaowed to Weed.

Weed stared up at the high stone wall. It seemed a long way to the top. She tensed her muscles. Then, pushing hard against the ground with her strong back legs, she leaped. She grabbed at the wall with her front paws and tried to pull herself to the top. But she hadn't jumped high enough. Disappointed, she slid to the ground.

"Start with a run," suggested Nutmeg, peering down at her.

Weed backed up a short way. With a deep breath, she took a flying leap at the wall. This time, she almost made it. Her claws scraped the top row of stones. But again, she couldn't hold on. *I'm just not big enough*, she thought miserably as she landed back on the ground.

Nutmeg blinked at her. "Try going further back," she miaowed.

Weed walked to the middle of the lawn. She turned and eyed the wall. Even from this distance, it looked too high for her. It wouldn't matter how fast or how far she ran. She wouldn't be able to jump to the top. She was just too small.

"I can't do it," she mewed to Nutmeg.

"You'll have to hunt without me."

"That won't be so much fun," miaowed Nutmeg.

"I know," agreed Weed. "But it's even less fun being so tiny!"

Nutmeg was about to join her sister on the ground when she spotted something moving in the shrubs on the other side of the wall. "A beetle!" she growled softly. She crouched, ready to spring.

Weed looked on enviously. Nutmeg's tail lashed back and forth as she waited for the right moment. Silently, she inched forward then suddenly disappeared as she dropped down to the other side of the wall.

Weed heard a thud and a scuffle. It sounded very exciting. Next, there came a quick scuttling noise. Had Nutmeg's beetle escaped? "I'm coming after you!" Weed heard Nutmeg growl at the beetle.

Weed waited for her sister to jump back into the garden. "Nutmeg?" she miaowed after a while. There was no reply. *She's probably chased the beetle far away*, thought

Weed. *I don't think she'll come back now.* She turned and headed back towards the flat. *I'll go indoors and see what Gran is doing*, she decided.

Before Weed reached the house, her little nose picked up the smell of something delicious. "Mmmm," she purred. "That smells just like Gran's special shortbread biscuits."

Gran made the most delicious biscuits and cakes. Sometimes she gave Weed a few crumbs to taste but that was never enough. Weed longed for a whole biscuit to herself.

She padded into the kitchen. The smell was mouthwatering. It was coming from the table in the middle of the room. There was no sign of Gran.

Oh good! thought Weed. *Now's my big chance.*

She stood up on her hind legs, trying to catch a glimpse of the biscuits. But she couldn't even see the top of the table.

I'm going to have to climb up onto it somehow, she told herself.

She padded about the kitchen, searching for a way to reach the biscuits. The armchair was still in front of the window sill. It was also quite close to the worktop. Weed worked out that she could jump onto the chair then up to the worktop. *And then I just have to leap across to the table*, she told herself. It wouldn't be long before she was munching a whole piece of shortbread. She could almost taste it already!

The first part of her plan was easy. In two leaps, Weed was on the worktop. At last she could see the biscuits. There were lots of them. They were lying on a rack to cool down.

Weed licked her lips. She faced the table and bent her hind legs. "Here goes!" she miaowed, throwing herself forward with all her might. She sailed through the air, stretching her front legs out as far as she could.

For a split second, her claws brushed the rim of the table. They hooked onto something hard and then she felt herself sliding backwards. "Help!" Weed howled, closing her eyes as she fell to the floor.

Clatter! *Bang*! Something crashed to the ground with her. Weed opened her eyes to see an empty baking tray lying next to her. *That's what my claws hooked into*, she thought.

"What's happened?" Gran came bustling into the kitchen. She chuckled when she saw Weed standing guiltily next to the tray. "I think I know what you've been up to," Gran said. "Just as well you couldn't jump much further. You might have pulled down all the biscuits too!"

"If I had, I could have eaten them," miaowed Weed. She was cross that her attempt had failed.

Gran broke a corner off one of the biscuits. "Here, little one," she said, putting it on the floor beside Weed. "You deserve something for your effort."

"Thank you," purred Weed. "But I really wanted a whole one."

Gran took a tin out of a cupboard and packed the biscuits into it. "I'd better put them away before I go to work," she said.

Weed watched sadly as Gran shut the shortbread inside a high cupboard. "I'll never be able to reach them there," she mewed.

Later that day, Weed decided to meet Gran at the lollipop crossing. *At least I don't have to jump onto anything to get there*, she thought as she ran along the pavement.

Weed turned the corner. Ahead of her, she could see Gran walking out into the middle of the road with her lollipop-shaped sign. The traffic stopped and a crowd of children crossed the road. Weed arrived just as the children stepped onto the pavement.

"Hello, everyone!" miaowed Weed, looking up at them.

But no one spotted the tiny ginger kitten at their feet. In no time at all, Weed was surrounded by all of the children. Some of them started to run. Weed had to dart out of the way as one big boy ran straight towards her. His heavy shoes just missed stamping on her. *That was close*! thought Weed. She trembled at the thought of being crushed under the boy's feet.

Gran still had to help a lot of other children who were waiting to cross the road. But Weed had had enough. *I'm going home*, she decided. She didn't want to risk being trodden on again.

She scampered home quickly. At the garden gate, she met her friend Duchess, a huge tabby who lived next door.

"You're in a hurry," miaowed Duchess,

who was sitting in the sun, cleaning herself. "What's the rush?"

"Oh, nothing," replied Weed gloomily. She sat on the pavement next to Duchess. "It's just that I've had such a bad day. Everything I've wanted has been out of reach and just now a boy nearly trod on me."

"Don't worry, Weed," Duchess miaowed kindly. "I'm sure you'll have better luck tomorrow."

"I don't think so," Weed mewed sadly. "You see I'm just too tiny." She looked up at Duchess who seemed to tower over her. Weed felt smaller than ever. "I wish I could be big like you," she miaowed. "Then I could do whatever I wanted."

2

The next morning, Weed ran out into the garden to play. Duchess was sitting on the wall, basking in the sun.

"Hello, Duchess," Weed miaowed. "Would you like to come exploring with me today?"

"That sounds like a good idea," miaowed Duchess, jumping down into Weed's garden. "I haven't been anywhere for a long time.

I've been feeling very lazy."

Weed blinked at her. "That's because it's so nice to lie in the warm sun," she mewed, slipping through the bars of the gate.

Duchess tried to follow Weed through the gap but it was too narrow for her. "Wait for me, Weed!" she miaowed.

Weed stopped and watched as Duchess sprang lightly onto the top of the gate then dropped down onto the pavement beside her.

"I wish I could do that," Weed mewed enviously.

"You didn't have to," miaowed Duchess. "You fitted through the gate easily."

The two cats set off along Liberty Street. "Let's visit Jet," suggested Weed.

Jet was one of Weed's brothers. He lived at the corner shop with Angie and Steve and their baby, Jill. The shop was a very interesting place – especially as mice sometimes lived in the storeroom! Once, Jet had caught a mouse so Steve named him Chief Mouser. Weed liked prowling around with her brother looking for mice. She hoped that one day she would catch one too. Then she could be Second Chief Mouser.

Angie was sweeping the front doorstep when Weed and Duchess padded up to the shop. "Hello, you two," she said, bending down to stroke them. "Have you come to play with Jet?"

"Yes," miaowed Weed. "And to hunt for the mice!"

Angie leaned the broom against the wall and picked Weed up. She held Weed in front of her and smiled. "You're turning into such a pretty little cat," she said.

"But I'm *too* little," mewed Weed.

"And your green eyes look beautiful against your orange coat," Angie went on.

Weed blinked. No one had ever told her she had lovely eyes.

Angie put her down and stroked Duchess. "As for you, Duchess," she grinned, "you're growing bigger by the day!"

"I wish *I* was!" miaowed Weed.

Angie straightened up and said, "I'm not

sure where Jet is today. Perhaps he's in the storeroom at the back. You'll have to see if you can find him there."

Weed and Duchess walked through the door. There was only one customer in the shop – a woman with her little boy. She was at the counter paying for her shopping. The little boy spotted the two cats and called to them. "Come, kitties. Here's a biscuit for you."

Biscuit! Weed's ears pricked up. *I wonder if it's a whole one*! She ran towards the boy who knelt on the floor and held out his hand.

"I like biscuits too," miaowed Duchess, running over with Weed.

The woman heard Duchess miaow and turned round. She frowned when she noticed the two cats approaching her little boy. Duchess was the first to reach him. She sniffed at the biscuit in his outstretched hand.

"Hey!" shouted the woman suddenly. "Leave him alone."

Duchess backed away and flattened her ears. "Why?" she miaowed crossly. "I'm not going to hurt him."

The woman clapped her hands together noisily in front of Duchess. "Shoo," she said. "Go away! You're too big. You'll hurt Peter with those huge teeth and claws."

"I won't!" protested Duchess. "I'm very gentle really."

"And don't snarl at me like that," said the woman, sternly. She gave Duchess a poke with her umbrella.

"Ouch!" yowled Duchess. "You're hurting me!"

The woman waved her umbrella in front of Duchess.

"All right, I'm going," hissed the big tabby, and she turned and ran out of the shop.

Alarmed, Weed sank back against a rack of magazines. She hoped the woman wouldn't see her and chase her away too. The umbrella looked dangerous with its spike at the end!

But the woman *did* see her. "Oh, look!" she said, crouching down in front of Weed. "Aren't you a tiny little thing!" She put down her umbrella and smoothed Weed's fur. "I hope I didn't frighten you," she said kindly.

Weed purred softly. "Not really. But you did frighten my friend," she mewed.

The woman turned to Peter. "Look at this sweet little kitty," she said. "Why don't you give her one of your biscuits?"

"But that's what he was doing when you chased Duchess away!" protested Weed.

"Oh dear, listen to her miaowing. I think she's hungry," said the woman. She picked up Weed and carried her over to Peter.

The little boy broke off a piece of biscuit and offered it to Weed.

"Mmm. A cheese biscuit," purred Weed, sniffing at it. She took it from him gently and crunched it up.

"Isn't she dainty?" said the woman with a smile. "Give her some more, Peter."

This time, Peter didn't break the biscuit first. He put a whole one on the floor in front of Weed.

"Oh good! A *whole* biscuit to myself at last," purred Weed as she tucked into the treat.

The woman chuckled. "You're the

prettiest cat I've ever seen. And what beautiful green eyes you have. Your owner is very lucky indeed!"

Weed stood up and flicked her tail proudly. "Do you really think so?" she purred happily. She looked across to the door and saw Duchess standing outside looking very miserable.

"I have to go back to my friend now," miaowed Weed. She looked up at the woman. "Just because Duchess is so big doesn't mean she will hurt you."

As Weed ran to the door, she heard the woman saying to Angie, "Well fancy that. Such a tiny kitten going around with that big, fierce-looking tabby!"

Outside, Weed nudged Duchess with her nose. "The biscuits were delicious," she told her. "I wish you could have had one."

"So do I," grumbled Duchess. "I don't know why that woman didn't like me. I didn't even show my claws."

"She said you looked fierce," Weed miaowed.

"I'm not fierce," miaowed Duchess, sounding cross. "I can't help being big."

Weed tried to cheer her up. "I left some pieces of biscuit for you," she mewed.

Duchess looked tempted. She peered into the shop then turned round. With a swish of her broad tail, she miaowed, "I'm not going back in there – not while that woman's still there. I'll find my own snacks." She started off down Liberty Street again.

"OK," miaowed Weed, trotting fast to

keep up with her friend. "Let's find some birds to chase. We might catch one."

Just down the road from the shop was a big garden that was filled with shrubs, trees and flowers. Birds flocked to it to feed on all the insects and worms that lived there. Weed had always wanted to go hunting in the garden but had been afraid she would get lost on her own. Now that Duchess was with her, she felt a bit braver.

Weed squeezed under the gate. "It's fantastic in here!" she miaowed. The garden looked like a jungle. There were birds everywhere, even on the lawn. "I'll easily get one of those," purred Weed. She could see spying several blackbirds pecking for worms amongst the grass.

Clatter! *Thud*! Duchess leaped over the gate and landed next to her. The sudden noise startled the birds and they flew away.

"Sorry," Duchess miaowed. "I can't sneak through gates quietly like you can. Now I've chased all the birds away."

"That's OK," mewed Weed. "You

couldn't help it. They'll come back." She looked round the garden. A wheelbarrow was parked near the path. "Let's hide in there," she suggested. "If we keep very still, the birds won't spot us."

The two cats scampered up the path and leaped into the metal wheelbarrow. There was a loud thump as Duchess landed. Then the wheelbarrow began to tip over.

"Oh, no!" howled Duchess. "What have I done?"

The wheelbarrow toppled over onto its side. Weed and Duchess shot out, just as it hit the ground with a loud clang.

"There won't be *any* birds left now," miaowed Duchess.

"No birds!" howled Weed. "But there *is* a dog. Run!"

Out of the corner of her eye, Weed had spotted a big brown dog. He had been sleeping in the shade nearby but the noise of the falling wheelbarrow had woken him up. In a flash he was on his feet. He stared at the wheelbarrow and suddenly caught sight of the two cats. With an excited bark, he tore across the lawn towards them.

There was no time to waste. Weed could see that this dog wasn't friendly or playful. His tail stuck straight up in the air behind him and the hair rose stiffly on his back.

"Run, Duchess!" Weed miaowed at the top of her voice.

The cats streaked across the garden towards the hedge. Weed could feel the ground shaking beneath her as the snarling dog chased after them.

Duchess tore past her. "Hurry, Weed!" she howled. "He's catching up!"

Weed's heart thudded in her chest. She tried to go faster but her legs were too short. She couldn't run nearly as fast as Duchess with her long, powerful legs.

Duchess reached the hedge first and looked for a way through. Frantically, she raced along, trying to find a gap.

"Through here!" miaowed Weed, spotting a small hole at the bottom of the hedge. She slipped through easily.

"Phew!" Weed gasped as she came out into the peaceful garden next door. "That was close." She turned, expecting to see Duchess scrambling through behind her. But the big tabby wasn't there!

"Duchess!" Weed miaowed. "Where are you?"

"I can't get through!" wailed Duchess desperately from the other side of the hedge. "The hole's too small!"

Weed froze. She could hear the dog's footsteps pounding ever closer. "Push hard!" miaowed Weed. She crouched down and looked back through the hole.

Duchess's frightened eyes stared back at her. "I can't!" howled Duchess. "I'm trapped!"

3

Weed remembered what had happened the day before when she had wanted to get onto the table. She couldn't jump straight up so she'd had to think of something else. "Find another way," she called to Duchess.

"There isn't another way," came the frightened reply.

"There is," miaowed Weed. "Climb over!"

Duchess's eyes suddenly disappeared from

the gap. Weed held her breath. What if the dog had grabbed her and dragged her off? "Duchess?" she called anxiously.

Above her, Weed heard a scrambling noise. She looked up. A pair of grey legs and a broad, striped tail appeared at the top of the hedge.

"You made it!" miaowed Weed as the rest of Duchess came into sight.

Duchess clambered down the hedge. "That was horrible!" she panted. She flopped to the ground, exhausted. "Just as well you told me to climb over. I was so scared, I couldn't think what to do. That nasty dog was snapping just behind me. He'd have caught me if I'd been on the ground a second longer."

Weed shuddered. They'd both had a narrow escape but Duchess had been in the most danger. It must have been terrible to hear the dog snarling so close to her. *I'm lucky I made it through the hole so easily*, Weed thought.

The dog was still hunting for them on the other side of the hedge. Weed could hear him snuffling and snorting. The hedge rocked and shook as he tried to climb up in search of Duchess.

"He's not going to give up in a hurry," Weed miaowed, peeping through the hole again. She could see two huge brown paws on the other side.

"No, and I'm not waiting till he does," miaowed Duchess. "I've had enough bad experiences for one day. Let's go home before anything else happens to me."

Weed knew how Duchess was feeling. Yesterday, she'd felt the same way after the boy nearly trod on her.

They slipped out of the garden into Liberty Street. Duchess crouched low and looked up and down the road, just in case the dog had also come out.

"All clear," Duchess miaowed, when she was sure the dog was safely in his garden. "Let's go."

Gran's flat wasn't far away but by the time they arrived, Weed and Duchess were very tired.

"See you tomorrow, Weed," miaowed Duchess, turning into her own gate.

"Why don't you come home with me?" suggested Weed. "Gran's probably back by now. She'll give us something nice to eat and then we can have a nap."

"That sounds lovely," purred Duchess. "My owners won't be home until much later today."

Gran was in the kitchen making a pot of tea. She turned when she heard the cat-flap bang. "There you are, Weed! I've been worried about you," she said. Then she saw Duchess pushing her head through the flap. "Oh, I see you've brought your friend home for tea," Gran smiled.

"And biscuits, please!" miaowed Weed.

Gran poured boiling water into the teapot. "You've been out a long time," she said. "I saw you going off before I went out." She stirred the tea. "I wonder what the pair of you have been up to?"

Weed rubbed her head against Gran's ankles. "We've had a big adventure," she purred. "And Duchess got chased twice! First by a woman with an umbrella and then by a fierce dog."

Gran reached up and took two tins out of a cupboard. Weed stared up at her. "We're very hungry," she mewed, hopefully.

Gran chuckled. "I know what you're after!" She tapped the tin. "And I can't say no. Those lovely green eyes are enough to melt anyone's heart."

Weed blinked in amazement. Everyone was saying nice things about her today! She remembered how no one had wanted to give her a home at first because she was so small and scraggy. But now, people were saying things that made her feel quite special.

Gran put the tea things on a tray and went into the living-room. She sat down in her armchair and poured milk into two saucers. "Here you are," she said to Weed and Duchess, putting the saucers on the floor.

"Thank you," purred Duchess loudly. "I'm very thirsty after my narrow escape."

"Can we have a biscuit too?" mewed

Weed when the saucers were empty. She opened her eyes as wide as she could and gazed up at Gran.

Gran laughed. "You don't need to open your eyes that wide to get my attention," she said, taking the lid off one of the tins. "Now, would you like a biscuit?"

"Yes, please!" miaowed Weed and Duchess together.

Gran put a biscuit onto each of the saucers. Weed bit into hers. "Hey! It's not shortbread!" she miaowed in surprise. "It's a cheese biscuit – like the one Peter gave me in the shop." She turned to Duchess. "So you do get one after all!"

When they'd finished their snack, Weed and Duchess sat at Gran's feet. "I'm going to have a nap on Gran's lap now," mewed Weed. She loved curling up with Gran. Her lap was soft and warm.

Duchess yawned. "Me too. I'm really tired," she miaowed. She put her front paws on Gran's knee, ready to jump up.

"Oh no, you don't, Duchess," smiled Gran.

Gently, she pushed Duchess down to the floor. "You're a gorgeous cat but you're much too big and heavy to fit on my lap." She winked at Weed. "But you can come up," Gran said, lifting Weed onto her lap.

Weed settled down. She peeped over Gran's knees to look down at Duchess, who was trying to make herself comfortable at Gran's feet. *Poor Duchess*, Weed thought. *She hasn't had a very lucky day! But I have.*

As Gran smoothed her fur, Weed purred contentedly and thought about all the good things that had happened to her that day. She had learned that people liked her green eyes and that she could squeeze through narrow gaps when it most mattered. Perhaps she didn't want to be big after all.

And one more good thing about being little, Weed thought as she drifted off to sleep, *is that I'm the perfect size to curl up on Gran's lap!*

Also by Lucy Daniels

GINGER, NUTMEG AND CLOVE

Nine Lives 1

Lucy Daniels

Bracken, the Bradmans' cat, has given birth to nine adorable kittens. Nine very different personalities each need very special homes. Can the Bradmans be sure they've found the right owners?

Red-haired *Ginger* is fearless and nosy – will he settle in with Amy and her mother? Or will he be too much of a handful?

Long-haired *Nutmeg* is really naughty and her new owners don't know how to keep her out of trouble. Until one day Nutmeg's inquisitiveness teaches her a lesson . . .

Clove doesn't seem too happy in her new home – and she won't eat the food that Mr Miller is giving her. Then the most unexpected person comes up with a solution . . .

EMERALD, AMBER AND JET

Nine Lives 2

Lucy Daniels

Bracken, the Bradmans' cat, has given birth to nine adorable kittens. Nine very different personalities each need very special homes. Can the Bradmans be sure they've found the right owners?

Greeny-eyed *Emerald* wants to find out what her owner, George, does every day when he's out at work. But could her curiosity cost poor George his job?

Amber is a gorgeous golden tabby – but she's convinced she's a dog! Will she discover the advantages of being a cat?

Jet is thrilled with his new home – he gets so much attention from Angie and Steve. But Angie has news for Jet that may put his cute little nose well out of joint?

DAISY, BUTTERCUP AND WEED

Nine Lives 3

Lucy Daniels

Bracken, the Bradmans' cat, has given birth to nine adorable kittens. Nine very different personalities each need very special homes. Can the Bradmans be sure they've found the right owners?

Snow-white *Daisy* is adorable – but very very quiet. What will make Daisy miaow for the first time?

Everyone wants to play with *Buttercup*. But can she please everybody at once?

Scrawny little *Weed* is the runt of the litter – who will want her? The Bradmans despair, but is the answer closer than they think?

The Nine Lives Trilogy by

LUCY DANIELS

0 340 73619 4	GINGER, NUGMEG AND CLOVE	£3.50	❑
0 340 73620 8	EMERALD, AMBER AND JET	£3.50	❑
0 340 73621 6	DAISY, BUTTERCUP AND WEED	£3.50	❑

All Hodder Children's books are available at your local bookshop or newsagent, or can be ordered direct from the publisher. Just tick the titles you want and fill in the form below. Prices and availability subject to change without notice.

Hodder Children's Books, Cash Sales Department, Bookpoint, 39 Milton Park, Abingdon, OXON, OX14 4TD, UK. If you have a credit card you may order by telephone, our call team would be delighted to take your order by telephone. Our direct line is *01235 400414* (lines open 9.00 am–6.00 pm Monday to Saturday, 24 hour message answering service). Alternatively you can send a fax on *01235 400454*.

Or please enclose a cheque or postal order made payable to Bookpoint Ltd to the value of the cover price and allow the following for postage and packing: UK & BFPO – £1.00 for the first book, 50p for the second book, and 30p for each additional book ordered up to a maximum charge of £3.00. OVERSEAS & EIRE – £2.00 for the first book, £1.00 for the second book, and 50p for each additional book.

Name ....

Address...

....

....

If you would prefer to pay by credit card, please complete:
Please debit my Visa/Access/Diner's Card/American Express (delete as applicable) card no:

Signature ....

Expiry Date ....